www.HarcourtBooks.com

Library of Congress Cataloging-in-Publication Data
Hale, Bruce.
Chet Gecko's detective handbook (and cookbook): tips for private eyes and snack food lovers/as decoded by Bruce Hale.
p. cm.
1. Hale, Bruce—Characters—Chet Gecko—Juvenile literature.
2. Detective and mystery stories—Appreciation—Juvenile literature. 3. Private investigators—Juvenile literature.
4. Cookery—Juvenile literature. I. Title.
PS3558.A35625C47 2005
813'.54—dc22 2004028492
ISBN 0-15-205288-7

Text set in Caecilia
Designed by Liz Demeter

First edition
H G F E D C B A

Manufactured in China

Oh, all right.
Since you seem to be
reading it anyway...

TOP SECRET INTRODUCTION

All the time kids ask me, "Chet, how did you get to be a big-time private eye?" (Okay, maybe not *all* the time. But somebody asked me this once.) Truth is, it's harder than it looks.

Being a detective takes knuckles and know-how. It takes nerves of steel, a brain like a high-speed computer, and a body like a Greek god's.

Well, that leaves you out.

Buzz off, Natalie! I'm trying to write.

Pay no attention. That was just my partner, Natalie Attired, the nosy mockingbird. She forgot who's the author around here.

Notes

 Never take on a wacko for a client. It wastes your time and it annoys the wacko.

Now, where was I? Oh yeah. Being a PI takes street sense (and not just knowing what street you live on, but knowing what *happens* on that street). You've got to be able to talk with anyone—from preschooler to principal—and catch their drift.

A detective has to know how to tail a suspect without being seen, stare down boredom on a long stakeout, read paw prints, decipher a crime scene, and dance a mean mambo.

Not just any knucklehead can become a private eye. But in case some knucklehead wants to try, I feel I owe it to my public to write down how to be a detective— the Chet Gecko way.

In this book you'll find everything I've learned in my time as the finest lizard detective at Emerson Hicky Elementary.

Should be a short book.

Watch it, worm breath...

Come on, Chet. You're going to need my help to keep the story straight.

Notes

 Danger is my business, but dessert is my delight.

Hmm, maybe you've got a point.... But it's at the end of your beak!

Har-har-har. Clearly you need help with your jokes, too.

Anyhow, this book will cover snooping, shadowing, stakeouts, snacks, and other vital scoops. Snacks, vital? You bet. A great philosopher once said—

Wait, when have you ever listened to a philosopher?

Okay, umm...a mighty general once wrote?

And when have you read anything by a general?

Geez, you're worse than Mr. Ratnose. Fine.

Some famous old dead guy once said, "An army marches on its stomach." (I suspect he was a snake.) A detective depends on his stomach, too. After all, you've got to keep your strength up if you wanna play the game, and a hungry PI is a sloppy PI.

Notes

 What if the hokey-pokey really _is_ what it's all about?

That's why I've included a few of my favorite recipes in this book. You'll find some truly killer snacks, along with a healthy dish or two. (Satisfied, Mom?)

These treats, together with my helpful tips, will put you on the road to becoming a real private investigator. Or at least to becoming a real pain in the tuckus. Sometimes it's hard to tell the difference.

Important reminder: This is top secret information. Treat it with care. Keep it out of the hands of little brothers and sisters. I recommend that if someone discovers you reading this book, you eat it immediately. And don't forget the ketchup.

Yours truly,

Chet Gecko, Private Eye

Notes

My idea of a balanced diet is a cookie in each hand.

Best to eat before you even begin—you never know when you'll have an opportunity for a quick bite once you're on a case.

Chet Gecko's Number One Recipe

I thought I'd start you out with an easy one—and coincidentally, my all-time favorite treat.

PILLBUG CRUNCH CANDY BARS

(Ask a grown-up to help you with this.)
Makes 12 candy bars
Total preparation time: 1 hour and 10 minutes

7-oz. chocolate candy bar
¼ cup chopped almonds
¼ cup Cocoa Krispies (if pillbugs aren't available in your area)

Cooking Tools and Materials
cool-looking chef's hat
glass or ceramic bowl
microwave
spoon
¼-cup measuring cup
waxed paper
small tray
sharp knife
aluminum foil or colored foils for wrapping candy

Notes

Whoever said you can't have your case and eat it, too, never met Chet Gecko.

1. Put on the chef's hat and check yourself out in the mirror. If you don't look like a dork, proceed to step 2.

2. Break chocolate up into glass or ceramic bowl.

3. Heat in the microwave for 10 seconds, stir; heat 10 seconds more, stir; and continue to do this until the chocolate melts. Too much heat can make the chocolate burn, and then it won't melt. Also, be careful not to get water in the chocolate because that can keep it from melting, too. Whatever you do, treat that chocolate carefully, okay? I'm serious about this.

4. Stir until smooth. (That is, until the chocolate is smooth, not until you're smooth.)

5. Stir in the chopped almonds and pillbugs (or Cocoa Krispies). Try not to go stir crazy.

6. Put waxed paper onto a small tray.

Notes

A tough private eye can resist anything... except temptation.

7. *Spread the chocolate out to the edges of the tray. Put another piece of waxed paper on top. Smooth the top.*

8. *Put tray in freezer for 45 minutes.*

9. *Remove tray from freezer and peel waxed paper off the top of the chocolate.*

10. *Cut the chocolate into 12 small candy bars and wrap them in foil. Hide them from your little sister and eat as needed.*

After sampling a bar or two to fortify yourself, put on your detective hat and get ready. It's time to learn how to be a private eye.

Notes

If quitters never win and winners never quit, who came up with the saying, "quit while you're ahead"?

1

THE CUSTOMER IS ALWAYS A FRIGHT

» Dealing with Clients

Unless you're just snooping for kicks, you gotta have a *client*—someone who hires you to investigate. A client makes the difference between a detective and a nosy pest. (That, and the cool fedora hat.)

If you *are* just sleuthing for grins and giggles, skip ahead to the next chapter. But if you want to be a *real* PI, hang tough.

So how do private eyes get clients?

Well, you could advertise in the newspaper. Of course, most kids at Emerson Hicky Elementary don't read the newspaper.

Or you could try skywriting your message. But that costs big bucks.

Notes

 My workout philosophy has always been a simple one: No pain, no pain.

Or you could go around asking kids if they need any mysteries solved. That might work.

How do I find clients? Well...mostly, they find me. I've got a reputation around school for solving mysteries.

You've also got a reputation for eating too much and causing trouble.

True. But in the PI biz, that's a good thing.

Yeah, but whoever's reading this doesn't have a reputation.

Hmm. Good point.

Okay, so I don't really know how you get clients.

Let's pretend someone already wants to hire you. Next thing, you need to figure out what to charge her. I usually ask for fifty bucks a day, plus expenses.

And you never get it.

Yeah, but it doesn't hurt to ask.

Bottom line: Clients are cheapskates. Getting money from them is harder than taking Easter candy from a sugar-crazed kindergartner.

Notes

I like exercise. I could sit and watch other people do it all day.

Notes

 Who do you think put the "art" in "smart aleck"?

Whether you are paid fifty bucks, fifty cents, or a bucket of deep-fried roach nuggets (don't ask), you need to watch your step around clients. They're not always on the up-and-up. In fact, clients can be as full of curves as a weasel in a whirlpool, and slipperier than a pack of caterpillars in Crisco.

Watch yourself. You'll want to:

a. make sure they're telling the truth;

b. get some money in advance, in case they fire you; and

c. try to report to them as seldom as possible.

Hey! Reports are important.

Too much like schoolwork for me.

Hmm, now that I think of it, clients are a real pain in the keister. They're hard to find, they're tightfisted, and they'll lie as soon as look at you. Let's forget about them and move on to the cool stuff.

14

Notes

Principal Zero was the kind of guy who would stuff your mouth full of tardy slips, then paddle your behind for mumbling.

>>Cool Trick #1

Kids ask me, Chet, what's the best part of being a PI? Is it the glamour of high-profile cases? The satisfaction of catching crooks? The big bucks?

Hah! What big bucks?

I gotta be honest with you: it's the cool tricks. They put the *Gee!* in G-man, and I'll be sprinkling these tricks throughout the book.

Secret Codes Say you need to slip a note to your partner without the bad guys (or your teacher) understanding it. Hard? No way. Just send a note in code.

My favorite is the shopping list code. Here's how it works.

Create a normal-looking shopping list. Your partner will decode it by taking the first letter of each word on the list. But if there's a number in front of the word, then you take whatever letter the number tells you to.

Notes

Some people can tell what time it is by looking at the sun, but I've never been able to make out the numbers.

For example: 4 *apples* means to use the l from that word, but just the word *apples* means to use the *a*.

Got it? Okay, try to decipher the shopping list message below.

5 papayas
2 cockroaches
underwear
rutabaga

6 horseflies
lemon
yeast

3 crickets
sugar

7 earthworms
pillbug
egg
2 gnats

{message reads: your fly is open}

And the best thing is, you'll have the ingredients for a shoofly pie if you care to make one.

Notes

 Acting is all about honesty. If you can fake that, you've got it made.

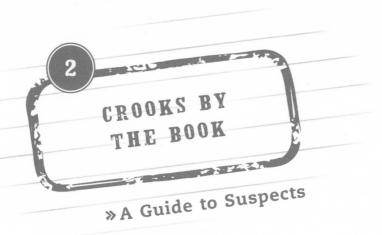

2

CROOKS BY THE BOOK

» A Guide to Suspects

What's a suspect? It's the guy you *suspect* might have done whatever bad deed you're trying to get to the bottom of. That's why they call 'em *suspects*.

Duh.

Duh, yourself. This writing stuff isn't as easy as it looks.

I've taken the time to give you the lowdown on some suspicious characters I've crossed paths with before. Some are known bad guys; some are just deeply weird. All of them bear watching.

Notes

The case was more tangled than a pair of pythons on a hot date.

Keep your eyes peeled for:

**HERMAN THE
GILA MONSTER**

punk Gila monster

Big, dumb, and ugly. Bad breath. Oh, and he's poisonous.

Good thing he's dumb as a stump.

MR. VIESÉL

weasel

Smooth as chocolate milk. Extortionist. Brilliant scientist and voodoo master.

Currently serving 5 to 10 years in Sing Sing for creating zombies without a license.

Notes

 A day without chocolate is like a day without sunshine. And a day without sunshine is like... night.

ALBERT LeGATOR

crocodile

Bad teacher. Very bad.

JACKDAW RIPPER

magpie

Light-fingered punk. Hangs out in rough company.

KNUCKLES McGEE

tomcat

Ruthless, tough, and a darn crafty principal impersonator.

Currently serving 10 to 20 in Walla Walla for trying to use a public school for private purposes.

19

Notes

If you toss a cat out of a car window, does it become kitty litter?

OLIVER SUDDON
screech owl

Science nerd and criminal mastermind. Hates disco.

BOSCO REBBIZI
ferret

Rude, crude, and really bad in math. Detention champ of Mr. Ratnose's class.

I thought you were?

ERIK NIDD
tarantula

A real sweetheart. Started the Dirty Rotten Stinkers gang.

20

Notes

 If a cow laughs, does milk come out her nose?

ROCKY RHODE
horned toad

Thug, shakedown artist, and all-around crook. Hopscotch champion two years running.

JOHNNY RINGO
raccoon

Emerson Hicky's best-known racketeer. Deals in all stolen goods; heck of a charming guy.

WALDO
~~prairie dog? wombat?~~
~~woodchuck?~~ furball

Amateur magician, wannabe detective. Still not sure about him.

Notes

 If I'm a nobody, and nobody's perfect, does that mean I'm perfect?

How to Spot a Suspect

Unfortunately for us private eyes, suspects don't stroll around with signs on their chests that read: GUILTY, GUILTY, GUILTY!

Except for Obvious Willie, the salamander.

Yeah, and it turned out he was innocent.

It's hard to tell most suspects from the usual crowd of teacher's pets, average students, jocks, brains, and cheerleaders that infests any school. But with luck and training, you can spot 'em. When asking questions, keep a lookout for:

- **Shifty eyes and nervousness:** This shows that whoever you're grilling has something to hide. And even if they're not guilty, they may know who is.

- **Opportunity and motive:** Were they near the scene of the crime when it happened? If it took place in a locked room, could they get their hands on the key? Do they have any strong reason for committing the crime?

Notes

 Being a private eye means taking lots of guesses and hoping they turn out right. But then, so does science class.

- **Punch in the jaw:** If someone I'm interrogating suddenly hauls off and bops me one, that's a good sign. Chances are they're connected to the crime.

Either that, or you ticked off another witness by asking obnoxious questions.

Sticks and stones, birdie. That's what you're gonna find in your cereal.

But spotting suspects is only the first step. After that, you've gotta figure out which one is the culprit.

How? Easy as stinkbug pie. Just look 'em dead in the eye and ask, Are you guilty? The trained detective can tell whodunit by their reaction.

Hah! You can't spot a culprit that way.

Nonsense. I do it all the time.

Notes

 Sometimes detective work can be harder than a week-old sowbug biscuit.

Oh, really? Name one case where you did.

Um...Well, there was...Uh...I'll get back to you on that.

Just in case you can't tell the culprit by looking in his eyes, let's cover interrogation techniques.

Notes

If it doesn't look <u>natural</u> and it doesn't act <u>super</u>, why do they call it <u>supernatural</u>?

Man, this writing is hungry-making. Time to break out another snack....

Hey, how about a birdie treat?

Be my guest.

You mean I should track mud on your floor, dirty your towels, and raid your fridge—like you do at my house?

Just give us the recipe, fluff-for-brains.

WORMY APPLE CRISP

(Get help from Mom or Dad with this one.)
Serves 6
Total preparation time: 1 hour and 45 minutes

Filling

4 large or 6 medium apples (about 8 cups sliced)

1 cup freeze-dried worms (chow mein noodles can be substituted if you're not crazy about worms)

½ cup brown sugar

1 Tbsp. ground cinnamon

1 Tbsp. cornstarch

Notes

 If you can pick your friends, and you can pick your nose...why can't you pick your friend's nose?

½ cup water

1 Tbsp. butter

Topping

6 Tbsp. butter, cold

1 cup flour

¼ cup sugar

¼ cup chopped almonds

2 Tbsp. water, cold

Herman the Gila Monster's so dumb, he can't make <u>water</u> without a recipe.

2 Tbsp. fresh bread crumbs (or 1 Tbsp. dried crumbs)

2 Tbsp. freeze-dried worms (or chow mein noodles)

1 batch of antennae from fresh martians

Chet, cut that out! no martians!

26

Notes

There are two theories on how to argue with a principal. Neither one works.

Cooking Tools and Materials

apple corer

carrot or apple peeler

knife for slicing apples

nonstick cooking spray

9 × 13 baking dish

small saucepan

1 set of measuring cups

1 set of measuring spoons

large stirring spoon

cheese grater

waxed paper

fork

Preheat the oven to 350 degrees.

1. *Core, peel, and slice apples.*

2. *Spray baking dish with nonstick cooking spray and fill dish with sliced apples and freeze-dried worms (or chow mein noodles).*

3. *Heat brown sugar, cinnamon, cornstarch, water, and butter in a small saucepan over medium heat. Stir until the sugar is dissolved (that's when it doesn't crunch against the bottom of the pan as you stir). Remove pan from the heat.*

4. *Pour sugar mixture over the sliced apples and freeze-dried worms (or chow mein noodles). Stir to mix them all together.*

5. *For the topping, grate butter onto a piece of waxed paper. Measure the flour, sugar, and chopped almonds onto the butter, then sprinkle the cold water on top.*

Sprinkling water? Don't be a drip.

Do you mind?

27

Notes

Let a smile be your umbrella...and you'll get a mouthful of rain.

6. Use a fork to moosh the flour into the butter—smashing and stirring just until the dough begins to form clumps.

7. With very clean hands (let me see under those nails, mister), sprinkle the clumps of topping around on the top of the apples.

8. Sprinkle bread crumbs and worms (or chow mein noodles) on top.

Worms? Ugh.

I'm not reading what you write. La, la, la...

9. Pop it into the oven to bake for 40 to 50 minutes or until the topping begins to turn golden brown and the apples sound bubbly (really more like a crackly sound).

Oh yeah, like you can tell the difference between bubbly and crackly.

10. Cool for about 10 minutes, then scoop onto plates.

Then, if you're not a bird, slide your plate into the trash.

How rude. That's the last time I share a recipe with you.

Promise?

Notes

 Trouble stuck to him like dumb on a dingbat.

3

DRESSED TO GRILL

» Interrogation Techniques

Whether you're grilling a suspect or trying to charm information from an innocent bystander, you've gotta know how to handle yourself in an interview. Ask the right questions; get the right answers. (Of course, this doesn't seem to apply to math tests. I'm doomed no matter what questions they ask.)

Here's the lowdown on squeezing the most from your question session.

Location

Ideally, you want to get your suspect in a small room and shine a bright light in his eyes. That way, when you ask questions, he'll break down and confess.

Notes

 Things are darkest just before...they go completely black.

But what if you're questioning an innocent witness?

Same thing.

Won't it make 'em clam up?

Hmm. Good point. Give 'em a comfy chair.

Unfortunately, we don't have many small rooms with bright lights at Emerson Hicky Elementary. In fact, there's only one—in Marge Supial's health office—and it ain't worth risking a wombat bite to use it.

30

Notes

Never take on a wacko for a client. It wastes your time and it annoys the wacko.

So make the best of things. Interrogate your suspect wherever you can. But try not to do it on the telephone. It's much easier to lie over the phone, as anyone who's ever called in sick will tell you. (Not me, of course, but I know kids who have.)

Making the Suspect Talk

Sometimes suspects just won't spill the beans. What do you do then? Whap 'em over the head with a wet silverfish? Nah, just bust out one of these three time-honored techniques.

1. The Bribe

Nothing greases the wheels like a well-chosen bribe. And you'll find that chocolate's the best wheel-greaser with most kids.

You mean, with you.

Well, duh. It's my book.

Notes

Danger is my business, but dessert is my delight.

But what if the kid is allergic to chocolate? What if he's on a diet?

All right, already. Don't be such a fussbudget.

The point is, use a bribe that motivates your suspect. Strangely enough, not everyone goes for chocolate. Some are moved by friendship, some by money, some by power, and some by big wet smooches.

Eeew.

Eeew is right. I had to get de-cootiefied after I wrote that.

When it comes to bribes, here's a good rule of thumb: Candy is dandy, but money is...expensive. Bribe 'em with bucks only if nothing else works, or you may have to send your piggy bank in for emergency surgery.

Here's a treat I've found really helpful in getting reluctant suspects to talk.

Notes

 What if the hokey-pokey really _is_ what it's all about?

BLOWFLY BANANA MUFFINS

(Ask your dad or mom to help with this.)
Makes 16 muffins
Total preparation time: 1 hour

Batter

2 cups flour

$\frac{1}{2}$ Tsp. baking soda

1 Tbsp. baking powder

$\frac{1}{4}$ Tsp. salt

$\frac{1}{2}$ cup butter (one stick), room temperature

$\frac{1}{2}$ cup sugar

2 large ripe bananas, mashed (1 cup)

$\frac{3}{4}$ cup milk, room temperature

1 egg, room temperature

1 cup chocolate-covered flies (if you're not a gecko, substitute chocolate-covered raisins and just tell your friends that they're flies)

Topping

$\frac{1}{3}$ cup flour

2 Tbsp. brown sugar

2 Tbsp. butter, room temperature

1 Tbsp. ground cinnamon

Cooking Tools and Materials

nonstick cooking spray

muffin tins (recipe makes 16 cupcake-sized muffins)

Notes

My idea of a balanced diet is a cookie in each hand.

plastic container with lid (holds 3 to 4 cups dry ingredients)

large mixing bowl

2 small bowls

one-quart jar with lid

1 set of measuring cups

1 set of measuring spoons

rubber spatula

potato masher

electric mixer (optional)

fork

Preheat the oven to 325 degrees.

1. *Spray inside of muffin tins with nonstick cooking spray. (Spray inside of mouth with whipped cream. Oh, we don't have whipped cream in this recipe? Never mind.)*

Notes

 Whoever said you can't have your case and eat it, too, never met Chet Gecko.

2. Measure the flour, baking soda, baking powder, and salt into a plastic container with a lid. Put the lid on the container and shake it up.

3. In a large mixing bowl, beat the butter into the sugar using an electric mixer, or if you're feeling especially beefy, smash it together and stir it with a rubber spatula. Really get tough with it—I'm not fooling here. The mixture should be soft and creamy when you're finished.

4. Mash the bananas in a small bowl with a potato masher (or use very clean hands to squeeze the bananas between your fingers—wait, you call those hands clean?) until the bananas are really smooshy.

5. Put the smooshy bananas into a one-quart jar with the milk and the egg. Put the lid on the jar REALLY TIGHT. Shake, shake, shake that jar—like a duck shakes his tail feathers at a disco—until the milk, banana, and egg become a yellowish slimy liquid. Eeew.

6. Using the electric mixer or a rubber spatula, beat some of the banana mixture into the butter mixture. Add half of the flour mixture. Stir in the rest of the banana mixture, then add the remaining flour mixture. Mix just until the white flour lumps disappear into batter.

7. Now stir the chocolate-covered flies (or raisins) into the batter. Using a $\frac{1}{4}$-cup measure, scoop the batter into the muffin cups. Don't fill the cups too full because the muffins will get taller as they bake, and you don't want to end up with mutant muffins on your hands.

8. Put the topping ingredients into a small bowl and use a fork (or very clean fingers) to rub the flour, sugar, butter, and cinnamon together until mixture is crumbly. Plop two teaspoons of this onto top of each muffin, then pile on any leftover topping. Lightly press the topping into the top of each muffin.

35

Notes

 A tough private eye can resist anything... except temptation.

9. Bake the muffins at 325 degrees for about 25 minutes. How do you know when they're done? Well, the edges will turn brown; the muffins will smell really yummy; and your suspect will suddenly become extremely cooperative. Another test: If you stick a toothpick into the center of a muffin, the toothpick won't be gooey when you pull it out (unless you stick it into a fly).

10. Be sure to let the muffins cool awhile before you bite into one because the flies (or raisins) get pretty hot when they're baking. And don't let your suspect chomp a hot muffin, either. You want your suspects friendly, not fried.

Notes

 If quitters never win and winners never quit, who came up with the saying, "quit while you're ahead"?

2. The Threat

Some mugs won't talk no matter how much candy or money you lay on them. These are the ones I call the tough nuts. And there's only one way to crack a tough nut: apply pressure. (That, or drop it from a great height. But I don't recommend this approach with suspects; they don't talk much afterward.)

I've found that the best pressure is a threat, which can come in all shades and flavors. Your approach depends on your suspect. When talking to someone who values her reputation, like teacher's pet Bitty Chu, threaten to expose her dark secrets to the whole school.

But what if you don't know her dark secrets?

Fake it. Everybody's got secrets.

If your suspect already has a bad reputation, like the punk ferret Bosco Rebbizi, you could promise to tell everyone he's a teacher's pet. And acting like you'll tattle to the principal, Mr. Zero, works with just about everyone.

Notes

My workout philosophy has always been a simple
one: No pain, no pain.

But what if your suspect is a hardened criminal? What if he's someone like Erik Nidd, who chews up vice principals like cricket gum and has a permanent chair in detention with his name on it?

Well, you could try threatening him with a sock in the kisser—if you have a death wish or enjoy having your limbs rearranged, that is. Or you could do what I do: abandon the interview and hope you get lucky later.

And if you're trying to grill someone like Herman the Gila Monster, good luck. He's too big to threaten, too mean to bribe, and too dumb to live. Actually, if your suspect is as dumb as Herman, there is one technique you can try....

3. The Trick

Assuming you're smarter than the suspect (always a dangerous assumption), you can trick them into giving you information. But you have to be slyer than a fox infiltrating the National Association for the Preservation of Chickens. Tricking goes something like this:

You: So, Herman, I hear you were part of that gang that stole bumper cars from the amusement park.

Herman: No way. Detective has hearing problem.

Notes

I like exercise. I could sit and watch other people do it all day.

You: I hear your ringleader is one of the biggest crooks at school.

Herman: Detective has cracked brain.

You: And after your leader sold the cars on the black market, each gang member got a hundred bucks for his share.

Herman: Hundred bucks?! Roger only give Herman fifty!

One problem with this technique: If you trick someone bigger than you and she notices, get ready to run. Most mooks don't like being tricked.

Yeah, like that time you fooled Rocky Rhode, and she tied your tail—

That's enough, beak-face.

How to Interrogate

But it's not enough to find a way to get the suspect blabbing. You must know why you're interviewing them in the first place.

Are you gathering information? Spreading false rumors? Trying to stir things up? Angling for a better grade?

Notes

 Who do you think put the "art" in "smart aleck"?

Your purpose determines how you grill the suspect. If you want to stir things up, you might drop some information that makes your suspect worried. Like this:

You: Did you hear that Principal Zero found some paw prints at the scene of the crime?

Freddy Nostrils: Er, you don't say.

You: Yup. And he took the paw prints to the cops.

Freddy: You don't say.

You: Uh-huh. Before long, they should be able to finger the bad guys.

Freddy: You don't say!

Your Partner: Where's Freddy going?

You: He didn't say.

If you're trying to gather information, consider these helpful tips:

- **Act friendly.** Suspects are more likely to share secrets with you if they think you like them. So relax. Make small talk.

  Right: Hey, how about that math test? Pretty rough, eh?

  Wrong: Gosh, up close you're uglier than three warthogs that ran into a brick wall.

- **Ask "how" questions.** With a shy suspect, try

Notes

 Principal Zero was the kind of guy who would stuff your mouth full of tardy slips, then paddle your behind for mumbling.

to get him to open up. Do this by taking it easy and asking "open-ended" questions.

Last time you got "open-ended," it smelled like bean burritos for hours.

I'm taking that pen away from you right now—

Right: How do you feel about Lili Padd?

Wrong: Do you hate Lili's guts worse than a fifty-page report on 101 uses of lima beans?

- **Read the subject.** Some folks you can read like a book—the kind with few words and lots of pictures. Some folks are harder to read than a martian dictionary. Either way, try to figure out what motivates your suspect. Is he or she eager to please? Does she or he like money, fame, what? Give 'em what they want and they'll open up.

Interrogating Dos & Don'ts

- *Do* sit or stand close enough to hear the subject talk.
- *Don't* sit in her lap.
- *Do* use a soothing voice and look in her eyes.
- *Don't* hypnotize him to sleep.

Notes

Some people can tell what time it is by looking at the sun, but I've never been able to make out the numbers.

- *Do* interview the subject in person (or in *animal*, as the case may be).
- *Don't* interview him over the phone (unless he has really, really bad breath).
- *Do* let the subject blab on and on.
- *Don't* interrupt to tell a fascinating story about your aunt Chimpula and her hernia operation.
- *Do* act like you're interested.
- *Don't* sit and yawn or pick your nose (unless you've got a seriously crusty booger).

And above all, when you're interrogating a suspect, expect to hear lies. The worst crooks will lie just to keep in practice. And even the best people will lie to protect themselves.

You've told a few whoppers yourself.

Me? Never.

That's one, right there.

A private eye is a keen student of animal behavior. So when you're interrogating, pay close attention to the subject's face and body language. Sometimes they can tell you more than their words—especially if the subject is lying.

Notes

 Acting is all about honesty. If you can fake that, you've got it made.

Here's what to look for:

eyes: Rapid blinking or avoiding contact means liar. Closed eyes means you're boring the suspect.

face: Blushing means stress, shame (or that the suspect has a crush on you).

mouth: Biting nails means nervousness.

throat: Excessive swallowing means tenseness (or peanut-butter sowbug brittle for lunch).

smile: broad = friendly
too tight = suspect is faking it

sweating: means nervousness (or you're standing in the kitchen)

arms: Crossed means defensive.

fist: Clenched means you should duck.

hands: open = friendly
clammy = scared
touching mouth = lying
finger up nose = major-league booger

shoulders: Hunched means "leave me alone."

fidgeting: means fear (or fleas)

legs: Ankles locked means withholding information. Spread wide means open, nothing to hide.

tail: Twitching means jitters or ready to attack (in cats).

Notes

The case was more tangled than a pair of pythons on a hot date.

cap
(out of style)

ears
(full of wax)

muscles
(watch out)

eyes
(dull, shifty)

mouth
(drooling,
etc.)

hands
(beware
of booger
flicks)

legs
(not as stinky
as feet)

tail
(or lame
excuse
for one)

claws
(never
trimmed)

Notes

 A day without chocolate is like a day without sunshine. And a day without sunshine is like... night.

>>Cool Trick #2

The Old Newspaper Trick Ah, newspapers—the best PIs use 'em as cover while keeping an eye on a suspect. (Just make sure you're old enough to read, or it'll look suspicious.)

If you're facing the suspect, use a newspaper with a small spy hole cut into it. She won't even notice you're looking. (That is, unless you cut the spy hole in the paper as she watches.)

Notes

 If you toss a cat out of a car window, does it become kitty litter?

If you're sitting with your back to the target, paste a small hand mirror—the kind you'd find in your mom's purse—on the paper. You can watch suspects to your heart's content, and they won't suspect a thing!

Make sure to get Mom's permission before taking the mirror.

Geez, you're such a worrywart.

Notes

 If a cow laughs, does milk come out her nose?

4

SNEAK FOR YOURSELF

» How to Follow without Getting Caught

Being a private eye calls for lots of sneaking around. Of course, this is also true of avoiding chores at home, so I get plenty of practice. When you're sneaking around after someone and trying not to be seen, we call this *surveillance*. *Surveillance* comes from the French word *surveiller* (meaning "hiding behind a fake schnozzola").

That's not what surveillance means.

It isn't? Pity.

There are two types of surveillance: chocolate and vanilla. (Oh, wait—that's milk shakes.) Anyway, you

Notes

 If I'm a nobody, and nobody's perfect, does that mean I'm perfect?

can spy on folks without moving, which we call *stationary.*

Like the paper you have to write thank-you notes on, but spelled differently.

Smarty pants.

Or you can do it on the hoof, which we call *shadowing* or *tailing.* Let's cover shadowing first.

The main rule of shadowing—and cheating on a spelling test—is: Don't get caught. (Not that I'd know anything about cheating on spelling tests....) No matter how you do it, stick with your subject, but don't let him or her see you. Be like a shadow—always there but never noticed.

Why shadow suspects? Lots of reasons:

a. to catch them in the act of a crime;

b. to get information about them;

c. to get them to lead you to someone else;

d. to prevent a criminal act; or

e. just because it's fun to sneak around.

The key is to blend in with your surroundings. If you're not a chameleon, this could be a little tricky, but

Notes

 Being a private eye means taking lots of guesses and hoping they turn out right. But then, so does science class.

it's not impossible. Just try to look like everyone else who has business being there.

At a school, dress like a student. At a mall, dress like a surly teen. At a clown convention, dress like a bozo. In short, blend in.

Blending in: Wrong way to dress while shadowing at school.

Notes

Sometimes detective work can be harder than a week-old sowbug biscuit.

Once you get the look right, focus on your behavior.

Funny, that's just what Mr. Ratnose keeps telling you.

Ha, ha.

How to Act

When you creep around like someone trying out for the movie role of Creeping Boy, your subject will be onto you quicker than an orca at an all-you-can-eat sushi bar. If you're lucky enough to have been born a gecko, you can crawl along the wall above your suspect and never be seen. If not, follow these tips:

- **Back off, Jack.** When you're right on your suspect's heels, not only will he notice you but you'll bump into him if he stops short. Leave at least a half block between you and your target.

- **Don't stare.** If you keep gazing at your suspect like she's the last velvet-ant fudge bar on the plate, she'll probably get suspicious. Glance, then look away.

Notes

If it doesn't look _natural_ and it doesn't act _super_, why do they call it _supernatural_?

- **Take cover.** Keep an eye on nearby bushes, trees, passing teachers, and doorways. You never know when your target will turn around, and you might have to hide in a hurry.

- **Act normal.** Carry schoolbooks (but don't look at them—that's too unnatural). Or, if you want to travel light, bring a newspaper and pretend to read it every now and then.

- **Excuse yourself.** If someone (like a teacher) asks what you're doing in the area, have a reason ready. (One of my favorites is "I'm working on a top secret story for the *New Jerk Times*.")

- **Disguise is wise.** If the subjects know you, you'll need a disguise. For the dumb ones, just a pair of shades or a hat will do. For the smarter ones, try something fancier, like Groucho glasses and a blond wig.

- **Bring plenty of moolah.** Have money and change ready, in case your suspect jumps onto a bus and you need to follow. (Or in case you get hungry and have to hit a vending machine for a Three Mosquitoes candy bar—which happens more often than you might think.)

Of course, shadowing is easier to do with two. That's why it helps to have a partner.

Notes

If you can pick your friends, and you can pick your nose...why can't you pick your friend's nose?

Aha! I knew you'd finally admit you need a partner.

Don't let it go to your head.

When you use a two-person surveillance team, it's harder for the suspect to lose you. Plus, if the target begins to sense he's being tailed, you can swap places with your partner. You can team-tail your subject in two ways:

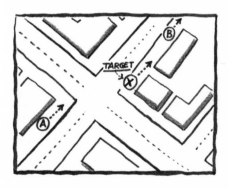

1. The Suspect Sandwich: One of you goes in front of the target and one follows behind. Sometimes the one in front can use a mirror (see Cool Trick #2) to keep track of the suspect. If the target reverses direction, the lead shadower becomes the back shadower. (This works best if you have walkie-talkies.)

Notes

There are two theories on how to argue with a principal. Neither one works.

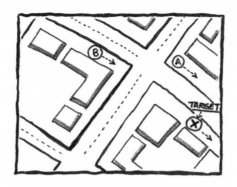

2. Follow the Leader: One of you takes the A position, behind the suspect. The second detective takes the B position, behind the first detective. If you think the target may have spotted the tail, A stops and lets B pass him. Then A drops into the B position. Repeat as needed.

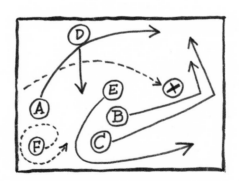

If you have three or more agents following a suspect, things get even fancier.

Notes

 Let a smile be your umbrella...and you'll get a mouthful of rain.

How come you can't write this clearly on science tests?

Is science more fun than detecting? I don't think so.

Getting Seen—on Purpose

Once in a rare while, you actually *want* to get spotted. (Of course, if you're a leopard, you're always spotted, but never mind that....) Sometimes, you want the suspect to know you're following him.

This is called turning up the heat. If they know you're on their tail, they could get nervous and flustered and make mistakes. Want an example? Take the case we call Moldy Socks for Breakfast. Natalie and I were shadowing a girl on the way to school, being obvious and hoping to startle her into making a goof.

The way I remember it, you accidentally tripped on a rake and knocked over a line of trash cans.

Notes

 Trouble stuck to him like dumb on a dingbat.

Hey, what are you gonna trust—your memory or my story?

Anyway, when she saw me on her tail, the girl got spooked. She led Natalie right to the moldy-sock thief—after she had claimed not to know the guy.

Yeah, but she would've gone to him anyway. She was in his class.

Are you gonna quibble over details all day?

The point is, it worked. Sometimes you gotta be seen to get the job done.

Notes

Things are darkest just before...they go completely black.

When you're shadowing someone, you'll want to keep your strength up. It's best to bring snacks, like this one, that aren't too crunchy or gooey.

BOLL WEEVIL BISCUITS

(Remember to ask Dad or Mom for help with this.)
Makes 12 biscuits
Total preparation time: 35 minutes

½ cup butter (1 stick), cold
2 cups flour
1 Tbsp. poppy seeds (or baby boll weevils, if available)
2 Tsp. baking powder
½ Tsp. salt
½ Tsp. baking soda

1 egg, room temperature
6 Tbsp. plain yogurt, room temperature

Cooking Tools and Materials

grater (and the greater the grater, the better)
1 set of measuring cups
1 set of measuring spoons
fork
medium bowl
small bowl
cookie sheet

Notes

Never take on a wacko for a client. It wastes your time and it annoys the wacko.

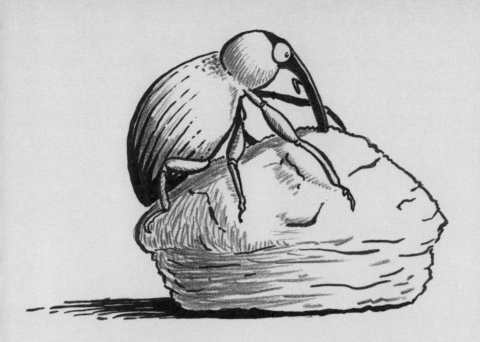

nonstick cooking spray

electric nose-hair trimmers (What? We don't need those? Never mind.)

Preheat the oven to 400 degrees.

1. *Grate the butter into a medium bowl. Watch out for your fingers— grated fingers ain't so tasty.*

2. *Measure the flour, poppy seeds (or boll weevils), baking powder, salt, and baking soda onto the top of the grated butter.*

3. *Use a fork to moosh the flour into the butter, like a bully mooshes his favorite victim.*

4. *With very clean hands, rub the butter bits between your thumb and the tips of your fingers, until the mixture is crumbly. (Of course, if you have paws, this might be a little tricky.)*

Notes

 Danger is my business, but dessert is my delight.

5. Break the egg into a small bowl and stir in the yogurt. Add this mixture to the flour mixture and stir until it all clumps together.

6. Spray the cookie sheet with nonstick cooking spray.

7. Take about 2 Tbsp. of dough and roll into a ball like an armadillo (but not quite so big). Put onto the cookie sheet and flatten the top with a fork. Repeat until you fill the sheet.

8. Bake at 400 degrees for about 15 minutes, or until the tops are lightly browned. (If the biscuits end up as black as a gorilla's armpit, you'll know you've cooked them too long.)

9. Let cool. Stuff your face.

Notes

 What if the hokey-pokey really _is_ what it's all about?

5
BREAKIN' OUT THE STAKEOUT

» Setting Up a Surveillance

What do you call it when you do surveillance while just sitting around on your duff?

Bone lazy?

Nope, we call it a stakeout. If you want to catch someone in the act, there's no substitute for it.

On a stakeout, your main problems are the two Bs: boredom and bathroom breaks. Sometimes a PI has to hang out in an uncomfortable place for a long time to get the goods on a suspect. Like the time I spent three hours in a pile of dirty laundry in the boys' locker room.

Yuck. You still stink from that.

Notes

 My idea of a balanced diet is a cookie in each hand.

No, I think that's your Wormy Apple Crisp.

Oh, you're a riot.

Anyhow, the best way to approach a stakeout is to get organized. Planning ahead can eliminate plenty of problems.

Pick Your Spot (Not Your Nose)

The first key to a good stakeout is finding the right spot. You want to see but not be seen (much like a truant officer). I always find it helpful to scout out the area before the stakeout starts.

Look for a place that offers good cover but lets you see what's going on. Here are some dandy surveillance spots:

- restaurant table
- detention hall
- behind parked car (if it belongs to your family)
- rooftop
- building next door
- bushes (but watch for thorns!)
- Dumpster (but only if you're desperate)

Notes

Whoever said you can't have your case and eat it, too, never met Chet Gecko.

The best spot for your stakeout depends on what you're trying to watch. Go for comfort if you can, but don't get too comfortable.

Yeah, remember your brilliant stakeout in the mattress factory? The suspect got away.

Look on the bright side: At least I caught up on my sleep.

Notes

A tough private eye can resist anything... except temptation.

Beating Boredom

The hardest part of a stakeout is staying alert as the hours pass and Ol' Man Boredom comes to visit. As my grandpa used to say: Always be alert; the world needs more *lerts*.

There are three ways to defeat boredom and stay alert on stakeout,...and I have no idea what they are. No fooling—if you have any brainstorms, let me know. I've tried biting the inside of my lip, slapping myself, and silently singing "99 Bottles of Beer." Nothing works.

What to Bring on a Stakeout

A well-prepared detective is a happy detective. When I'm on a long stakeout, these things come in handy:

- snacks
- a disguise
- newspaper with a hole in it (for spying)
- snacks

Notes

 If quitters never win and winners never quit, who came up with the saying, "quit while you're ahead"?

- binoculars (if you can borrow from Dad)
- notebook and pencil (for notes)
- snacks
- napkins (for snacks)
- pin (for sticking yourself if you get sleepy)
- empty cup (for bathroom breaks)

Gross. Does your mom know you're writing this?

- sunglasses (to look cool)
- snacks
- comic books (for when you get bored)

You can't read a comic book on a stakeout.

Why not?

Remember when you missed that groundhog leaving his condo because you were so wrapped up in Funky Mystery Comix?

Oh. Yeah. Scratch the comic books.

Notes

 My workout philosophy has always been a simple one: No pain, no pain.

- electronic bugging device
- long-distance receiver
- night-vision goggles

Come on. Kid detectives can't afford all that. You don't even have that stuff.

Hey, a gecko can dream, can't he?

Observation and Memory Techniques

On stakeout, a good detective stands (or sits) ready— eyes and ears open. His success depends on luck, and on his powers of observation and memory.

That reminds me of a Sherlock Holmes story. Dr. Watson and Holmes go camping. They have a fine meal, set up their tent, then climb into their sleeping bags to sleep. In the middle of the night, Holmes wakes up, looks around, and nudges Watson. He says—

Is this gonna take long?

Put it on ice, birdie. I'm telling a story.

Notes

 I like exercise. I could sit and watch other people do it all day.

Anyway, Holmes says, "Look up, Watson. What do you see?"

Watson says, "Well, I see thousands and thousands of stars."

Holmes nods and says, "And what does that tell you?"

Watson thinks. Then he says, "I guess it means the sky is clear and we will have another nice day tomorrow. What does it tell you, Holmes?"

Sherlock Holmes says, "Watson, you fool. Someone has stolen our tent."

The point is, sometimes the hardest part of observation is noticing what's right in front of you. You can miss something because it's too obvious. (Of course, just because *you* miss it doesn't mean that *I* would. As an experienced detective, I have a memory like a steel trap and powers of observation stronger than the coffee in the teachers' lounge.)

Ha. You got lost on your own street once.

Yeah, but it was dark.

Notes

 Who do you think put the "art" in "smart aleck"?

Successful observation calls on all of our senses—sight, hearing, smell (some folks smell better than others), touch, taste, and humor.

Chet, humor isn't one of the five senses.

Oh yeah? Then why do we call it a sense of humor?

Most folks depend on just sight and hearing, but a keen detective employs as many senses as possible. How can you become a sharper observer? Well, you could stick your head in a pencil sharpener. Or you could try this memory-building exercise.

Look Sharp: An Observation Exercise

Sit someplace where you can watch the world around you but won't be interrupted. Pretend your eyeballs are a camera. Now take a mental picture of the scene (but be sure you've got film in your camera).

Close your eyes. Have a friend or partner ask you questions like:

Notes

Principal Zero was the kind of guy who would stuff your mouth full of tardy slips, then paddle your behind for mumbling.

- How many windows does the building have?
- How many rows of chairs are in the room?
- What color are my eyes?
- What does the teacher's dress look like?
- What is the average flying speed of a one-legged parrot from Paraguay?

How did you do? If your powers of observation are less than mind-boggling, try these two bonus exercises. Remember, the more you practice, the better you get.

1. Think of a place you see every day—your classroom, the house across the street, the principal's office. (Okay, maybe *you* don't see the inside of the principal's office every day.) When you're away from that spot, write down a detailed description of what it looks like. Check the description the next time you go to that spot. You'll be amazed at how much you missed.

2. Think of someone—a friend, a teacher, an enemy—you know well. When you're alone, sit down and write a full description of that person. Keep the description in your pocket. Next time you see the person, compare your notes and the person (but not out loud, unless you're hungry for a knuckle sandwich).

Here's a helpful tip: Whether on stakeout or not, always keep a pen and notepad handy. It's all hunky-dory

Notes

 Some people can tell what time it is by looking at the sun, but I've never been able to make out the numbers.

to have a dynamite memory, but even the best PI can't remember everything.

When checking out a scene, write down all the details you can think of, like...

- day, date
- location
- weather
- who's around
- sights and smells
- any interesting snacks
- relative cootie factor
- etc.

You never know which detail will turn out to be the important one.

Remember that time we caught the culprit because we wrote down the smell at the crime scene and his desk smelled exactly the same?

Ah, yes. Who would've guessed that an iguana would have a stinky cheese collection?

Notes

 Acting is all about honesty. If you can fake that, you've got it made.

What to eat on a stakeout? Ah, the possibilities are endless. Although I've munched everything from potato-bug crisps to leftover wolf-spider pizza, Mothcake Shortbread is a good old standby.

MOTHCAKE SHORTBREAD

(Get some help from a parent for this one.)
Makes 12 mothcakes
Total preparation time: 40 minutes

Shortbread Dough

¼ cup brown sugar
½ cup butter (1 stick), room temperature
1 cup flour
⅓ cup uncooked oatmeal (or moth wings)

Cooking Tools and Materials

1 set of measuring cups
fork
medium bowl
waxed paper
rolling pin
2-inch round cookie cutter
cookie sheet

Preheat the oven to 325 degrees.

1. *In a medium bowl, stir together brown sugar and butter with a fork. Mix well, even if they disagree with each other. After all, you're the boss.*

Notes

 The case was more tangled than a pair of pythons on a hot date.

2. Stir in flour and moth wings (oatmeal).

3. Put the dough onto a piece of waxed paper sprinkled with flour. Press it down with your hands so it sticks together in one lump. (And don't munch the raw dough—it doesn't taste so hot. I tried it.)

4. Sprinkle top of dough with flour and roll out with a rolling pin to about $3/8$- to $1/2$-inch thick.

5. Chop dough into circles with cookie cutter and put each circle onto the ungreased cookie sheet. Roll scraps together and cut out more circles until all dough is used up, or until your scraps get really, really tiny.

6. Bake for 25 minutes or until the edges are lightly browned.

7. Raw moths are pretty dry and hard to swallow, but mothcakes make a perfect snack for anyone on stakeout (especially if you remember to bring along some chocolate locust milk).

Notes

A day without chocolate is like a day without sunshine. And a day without sunshine is like... night.

>>Cool Trick #3

Pencil Mouth   Have to talk to a suspect on the phone but don't know how to disguise your voice? No problem. I use this trick all the time. Take an ordinary pencil and hold it in your teeth. Then talk. Guaranteed, the suspect won't recognize your voice. (Of course, make sure to put the pencil in sideways, not point first—otherwise your scream will make the suspect deaf.)

Notes

 If you toss a cat out of a car window, does it become kitty litter?

6
CLUE IN THE FACE

» The Finer Points of Snooping

Snooping is detective lingo for *searching for clues,* and searches demand a certain...well, snoopiness. It pays to be nosy if you're a detective. To solve mysteries, we have to poke our noses into all kinds of funky places. (Funkier than a camel's nostril after a ten-day desert trek.)

So where do you snoop for clues? Clues are all around us. Look on your dad's shirt—you'll find a clue about what he had for lunch. (Unless my nose deceives me, fungus-weevil pizza.)

If you're snooping into a teacher's doings, try desks, cars, and trash cans. If you're investigating a little sister, check under her bed or in her desk drawers.

Notes

 If a cow laughs, does milk come out her nose?

But wherever you nose around, remember the two Golden Rules of Snooping:

1. Don't get caught.
2. If you *do* get caught, deny everything.

Digging In

I usually like to start my search in the kitchen. Examine the inside of the fridge and the cookie jar with special care. Even if you don't find any clues, you'll often detect a cookie or similar treat that will give you extra energy.

Notes

 If I'm a nobody, and nobody's perfect, does that mean I'm perfect?

When searching, I try to put myself in the criminal's shoes (and hope he doesn't have athlete's foot). I ask myself: Where would I hide something if I didn't want anyone to find it? In past cases, I've found clues hidden:

- in desks
- in file cabinets
- taped underneath drawers
- in lockers
- inside toilet tanks
- behind framed pictures
- in candy stores

Wait a minute. What have you ever found in a candy store?

Um...candy?

Searching a Trash Can

Take it from someone who's learned the hard way: Teachers don't mind you searching their trash for clues—as long as they don't catch you at it. There are two schools of thought on how to search a trash can. Both of them are yucky.

Notes

Being a private eye means taking lots of guesses and hoping they turn out right. But then, so does science class.

First, there's the *plunge method*. Just take your hand and plunge it down into the middle of the trash, rooting around for something that looks important. Advantages: It's quicker and neater. Disadvantages: Sometimes you miss things, and your sleeves end up smelling like old tuna fish sandwiches.

Then there's the *dump method,* which takes great control and finesse. First, you spread a sheet, large garbage bag, or towel on a tabletop. Then dump the contents of the trash can on top of it. Advantages: A thorough search. Disadvantages: Not highly popular with parents or teachers—especially if your aim is so-so.

Searching a Crime Scene

There are three main ways to search a crime scene: the *Niña,* the *Pinta,* and the *Santa María.* (Just kidding.)

Trained detectives know these search patterns as the Grid, the Spiral, and Wandering Around Like a Doodlebug Hoping to Get Lucky. Each method has its supporters.

Notes

Sometimes detective work can be harder than a week-old sowbug biscuit.

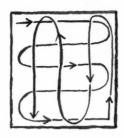

The Grid

Say you're searching the cafeteria for clues after a robbery. Using the Grid, you'd walk back and forth, from one wall to the opposite, until you cover the entire floor. Then you'd walk the room the other way from wall to wall, back and forth, until you'd covered the floor that way. (This method is for those who eat their Pillbug Crunch bars one square at a time.)

The Spiral

The Spiral search pattern is pretty much what it sounds like. Starting from the spot where the crime was

Notes

 If it doesn't look <u>natural</u> and it doesn't act <u>super</u>, why do they call it <u>supernatural</u>?

committed, you walk in an ever-widening circle, with your eyes sweeping the ground for evidence. Continue until you cover the entire floor (or until you get dizzy and toss your cookies, whichever comes first).

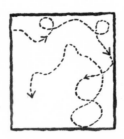

Wandering Around Like a Doodlebug Hoping to Get Lucky

This method is for those who believe that luck and pluck will help them more than the scientific method. Basically, you wander around aimlessly—looking at stuff, sniffing behind curtains, snarfing up stray muffins—until you get bored. I've solved more cases with this search method than with both of the other ones combined.

Notes

If you can pick your friends, and you can pick your nose...why can't you pick your friend's nose?

That's because you're too lazy to do an organized search.

Lazy? Please. I prefer "ambitionally challenged."

What do you find when you search? That's what we call *evidence,* and we'll talk about that right after a pause for the cause—snacks.

Notes

 There are two theories on how to argue with a principal. Neither one works.

Sometimes searching for clues can really give you an appetite.

That's what you said about shadowing and interrogating and—

And it's all true.

When I'm snooping, I like to bring along the gooiest and most outrageous snack known to detectives—the one that makes kindergartners so hyper, they go into orbit, the one we call...

Chet's recipes have gotten way out of hand. The editors and I have substituted something a bit healthier.

EARWIG CHOCOLATE DEATH

Try this one at your own risk!

1 tarantula, whole
2 cups earwig butt
3 Tbsp. earwax (p
1 Tsp. cricket ant
1 Tsp. garlic
5 cups brown su
7 cups white su
2 cups water
whole lotta bu

TICK TACO SALAD*

*Warning: Involves sharp knives. Only prepare this recipe under the supervision of a Ukrainian knife juggler, certified pirate, or other responsible adult.

Makes 12 to 15 servings

Total preparation time: 1 hour and 10 minutes

¼ cup olive oil

3 cloves garlic, minced (that means chopped into tiny pieces)

1 small onion, sliced really thin

79

Notes

 Let a smile be your umbrella...and you'll get a mouthful of rain.

1 gallon fudge

a dash of cinnamor

Preheat the oven to

1. Rip the tarantu
   legs off.

2. Combine tarar
   legs and earu

3. Add sugar.

4. Add more su

5. Pour water
   bowl.

6. Beat the e
   until crea

7. In a sepa
   bowl, mi

8. Throw t

9. Send yo

10. Bake a

11. Serve

---

1 Tsp. dried oregano (or 1 Tbsp. fresh)

2 Tsp. chili powder

1 Tsp. ground cumin

½ Tsp. ground black pepper

1 cup dried lentils (or ticks, if available)

2 cups long-grain rice

2 cups beef broth

3½ cups water

salt to taste

½ cup lettuce per person, torn into small pieces

vinaigrette salad dressing

¼ cup fresh cilantro, chopped (optional)

¼ cup grated cheddar cheese per person

¼ cup chopped tomatoes per person

1 large bag tortilla chips

Cooking Tools and Materials

large pot with lid

1 set of measuring cups

1 set of measuring spoons

large spoon for stirring and serving

serving plates

cheese grater (if not using shredded cheese)

joke book (to keep things lively while you're cooking)

1. Sauté the garlic and onion with olive oil in large pot.

Notes

 Trouble stuck to him like dumb on a dingbat.

2. Add the oregano, chili powder, cumin, and pepper. Then stir in the ticks (or lentils) and rice. Continue to stir until the rice is lightly browned.

3. Stir in the beef broth and water. Bring to a boil, then reduce heat and cover the pot. Let simmer for about 25 minutes, or until the liquid has been absorbed. This is a good time to read important jokes, like: What did the fish say when he hit a concrete wall? "Dam."

4. Remove the lid carefully to let the hot steam escape before you look into the pot. Stir the rice mixture and add salt to taste.

5. Toss the lettuce lightly with the vinaigrette salad dressing and spread some onto each plate. Put about ¼ cup of ticks (or lentils) and rice onto the lettuce. Sprinkle on a little cilantro (if you like cilantro).

6. Scatter grated cheese on top of the ticks (or lentils) and rice. Then plop down some chopped tomatoes around the edge. Break up some tortilla chips and sprinkle them on top.

7. Grab a fork and dig in. Be sure to thank your mom for remembering to look for ticks at the grocery store.

81

Notes

Things are darkest just before...they go completely black.

7
TRACK MAGIC

» Gathering Evidence

What is *evidence?* When your face is smeared with brown and your mom's trying to figure out who ate the last maggot fudge bar—that's evidence. It's a physical clue that helps you figure out whodunit.

Evidence can be as subtle as a scent in the air, or as obvious as a hijacked elephant in the backseat of a car. It's the PI's job to notice evidence wherever it turns up. That means keeping all your senses on full alert and your brain clicking at top speed.

If you did that just once in Mr. Ratnose's class, he'd keel over.

Which is why I don't do it.

Notes

Never take on a wacko for a client. It wastes your time and it annoys the wacko.

Evidence comes in all shapes and sizes. What you've gotta do is scope out all the information at a crime scene—paw prints, candy wrappers, mud pies, tire tracks, moldy orange rinds, half-eaten doughnuts, homework—and decide which of it is important. (Definitely the half-eaten doughnuts are.)

Learning to read a crime scene is like learning to read a schoolbook. At first a book is just a jumble of meaningless nonsense. Then, bit by bit, you study the alphabet, you improve your reading skills, you decipher the words on the page, and you find...it's just a jumble of meaningless nonsense. (Okay, bad example.)

Anyway, the point is you gotta learn how to *read* a crime scene.

Reading Tracks

These are the normal footprints of an average garden-variety gecko (although he *is* incredibly handsome). Notice the direction the feet point, the line left by the dragging tail, the distance between prints, and the even impression of heel and toes.

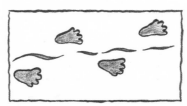

Notes

 Danger is my business, but dessert is my delight.

Now check out these trickier tracks and try to match them to the descriptions below:

A. toad hopping

B. fox running

C. bird dancing the hokey-pokey

D. T. rex with a limp

E. hippo on a pogo stick

1.

2.

Notes

What if the hokey-pokey really _is_ what it's all about?

3.

4.

5.

Answers: 1. A; 2. D; 3. E; 4. B; 5. C

Notes

 My idea of a balanced diet is a cookie in each hand.

Reading Fingerprints

Um...I know you're supposed to be able to pull the fingerprints off a glass and tell all kinds of stuff from them. Unfortunately, I still haven't gotten my mail-order Dr. Fingrito Fingerprinting Kit, so I couldn't tell you *what* kind of stuff.

Reading Clues

A crime scene offers a wealth of clues besides tracks and prints. How do you tell what's a clue and what's just junk? Beats me. I try to take in everything, writing careful notes in my pad. Then later I study those notes until I make a mental link with a suspect.

You, studying? Don't make me laugh.

Hey, as long as it's not a schoolbook...

It takes many cases and years of practice before you can read a crime scene as well as Natalie and me.

Notes

Whoever said you can't have your case and eat it, too, never met Chet Gecko.

Still, check out the evidence example below, and maybe you'll learn something.

(too tempting)

This brownie was found at the scene of a crime. See if you can guess which picture shows a brownie that's been there for: one hour; one day; three days; one week.

Notes

 A tough private eye can resist anything... except temptation.

Hmm. That diagram reminds me of something. Did I ever tell you the recipe for Ladybug Fudge? No? Then this is the perfect time.

LADYBUG FUDGE

(Remember to ask an adult for help with this.)
Makes about 25 pieces
Total preparation time: 4 hours and 30 minutes (includes 4 hours to chill)

Candy

14-oz. white chocolate candy bar or white baking chocolate

14-oz. can of sweetened condensed milk

dash of salt

½ to 1 cup Red Hots (or ladybugs, if they're in season)

Cooking Tools and Materials

glass or ceramic bowl

large spoon for stirring

microwave

can opener

1 set of measuring cups

waxed paper

9-inch square pan

X-ray glasses (Oh, we don't need these, either? Dang. I'll *never* get those glasses.)

1. *Break up white chocolate into glass or ceramic bowl. (If it's not broken up enough, tell it some sad stories.)*

Notes

If quitters never win and winners never quit, who came up with the saying, "quit while you're ahead"?

2. Heat in microwave for 10 seconds, stir; heat 10 seconds more, stir; and keep doing this until the white chocolate melts. Too much heat can make the chocolate burn, and then it won't melt. Also, be careful not to get water in the chocolate because that can also keep it from melting. Whatever you do, be careful with your chocolate. That stuff's like gold.

3. Stir until smoother than a sixth grader's lie.

4. Add the sweetened condensed milk and salt. Microwave 20 seconds at a time and stir just until chocolate and milk are well mixed.

5. Stir in the ladybugs (Red Hots), first making sure that none of them are still alive. (I just hate it when your ingredients get up and fly away.)

6. Line the square pan with waxed paper. Pour the fudge into the pan.

7. Chill until firm. Remove from pan, peel off the waxed paper, and cut fudge into squares.

8. Eat until bloated.

Notes

My workout philosophy has always been a simple one: No pain, no pain.

8

THE WHOLE SCOOP AND NOTHIN' BUT THE SCOOP

» Information Sources

It's not as fun as shadowing, it's not as exciting as grilling a suspect, but every detective knows that information gathering is a big part of the job. These days information is there for the asking (or buying). And the smart PI knows how to find it.

Where to start? Try your contacts.

Contacts? You mean you keep info on your eyeballs?

Not those contacts—I mean people, informants.

Notes

 I like exercise. I could sit and watch other people do it all day.

But then what about computer records and files and stuff like that?

Oh, okay, you can get information from *two* places: your contacts and public or private records. First, the contacts.

Contacts

These are folks it pays to get buddy-buddy with. They often can hold a key to the case, in the form of information that helps you solve it. It's harder to get information from contacts than from records because people can be rude, stubborn, and downright ornery.

And that's just your relatives.

You're a scream, birdie.

Sometimes you've got to flatter, bribe, or threaten your contacts to get them to talk. Once I even had to promise to be someone's valentine. *Yuck.* But the scoop I got was worth it. (After the de-cootiefication was over.)

91

Notes

 Who do you think put the "art" in "smart aleck"?

Once you develop contacts, it takes work to maintain them. Bring 'em a beetle-jelly doughnut every now and then; ask about their family; offer to do their homework.

You gotta act like the contact is your friend, even if her breath is strong enough to hold up a three-story parking garage. It can be a pain (being friendly with the contact, that is, not holding up the garage). But over the long run, contacts pay off with inside info you can't get any other way.

Here are some of the handiest contacts in my line of work.

- **Secretaries:** You think principals rule the school? Ha. Secretaries hold the real power behind the throne. They control most of the information at school, and you'd better stay on good terms with them if you want to learn anything.

  I regularly bribe our school secretary, Mrs. Crow, with worms and sowbug muffins—whether I need something from her or not.

- **Librarians:** Say you want to find out how to cure a zombie, or trap a werewolf, or even get an A on a book report. The librarian is your go-to guy (or gal). Every librarian might not be an expert in the supernatural like Emerson Hicky's own Cool Beans, but he or she will be a mother lode of other

Notes

 Principal Zero was the kind of guy who would stuff your mouth full of tardy slips, then paddle your behind for mumbling.

information. (Besides, librarians are actually *paid* to answer your questions.)

- **Nurses:** I try to visit the nurse as seldom as possible. (Maybe because she jabbed a needle in my tail the last time.) Still, a school nurse is your source for the lowdown on suspicious injuries, prescription drugs, and that funky rash that just won't go away.

What rash?

Never you mind.

93

Notes

Some people can tell what time it is by looking at the sun, but I've never been able to make out the numbers.

- **Gossips:** The great thing about gossips is, they love to talk about everybody's business. The bad thing about gossips is, they love to talk about *your* business. Go to them for the latest rumors and scuttlebutt, but don't tell them *why* you're asking, unless you want everyone in the school to know what case you're on.

  And remember, gossip is about as reliable as a tissue-paper hat in a hurricane. Trust it at your own risk.

- **Snitches:** A snitch is a fuzzy critter with a star on its belly and a—oh, wait, my mistake. That's a *sneech*. A snitch is someone on the wrong side of the law who'll spill his guts for a price. That price could be money, a treat, or a threat.

  Snitches aren't always trustworthy; in fact, they could double-cross you at any time. But they know what's happening in the world of crooks.

Remember when Stu Pigeon sold us out to those snack smugglers?

Yup. I never knew a Twinkie could work so well in hand-to-hand combat.

94

Notes

Acting is all about honesty. If you can fake that, you've got it made.

Trying to stay on the sweet side of a contact? I recommend a slice—heck, even a whole round—of Sweet Potato-Bug Pie.

SWEET POTATO-BUG PIE

(Ask a grown-up to help you with this.)
Makes 9-inch pie
Total preparation time: 1 hour and 30 minutes

Crust

6 Tbsp. butter, cold

1 cup whole wheat flour

$\frac{1}{4}$ cup Rice Krispies (or crunchy bug shells)

3 Tbsp. sugar

$\frac{1}{8}$ Tsp. salt

2 Tbsp. cold water

Filling

15-oz. can of yams in syrup (or sweet potato-bug puree, if your store stocks this)

$\frac{1}{2}$ cup brown sugar

1 Tbsp. ground cinnamon

$\frac{1}{2}$ Tsp. ground nutmeg

$\frac{1}{2}$ Tsp. ground allspice

dash of salt

2 eggs, room temperature

5-oz. can evaporated milk

1 can whipped cream

Notes

 The case was more tangled than a pair of
pythons on a hot date.

Cooking Tools and Materials

9-inch pie plate

grater

1 set of measuring cups

1 set of measuring spoons

fork

can opener

large bowl

potato masher (or potato-bug masher—either will do)

electric mixer

Preheat the oven to 350 degrees.

1. *Grate cold butter into pie plate. Contemplate. Lick a skate. Hibernate.*

Chet, put down that rhyming dictionary!

Notes

 A day without chocolate is like a day without sunshine. And a day without sunshine is like... night.

2. Measure whole wheat flour, Rice Krispies, sugar, and salt onto top of the grated butter.

3. Use a fork to smoosh the flour mixture into the butter mixture. With very clean hands rub the bits of butter between your thumb and fingertips until the flour becomes crumbly.

4. Add the cold water and mix all with a fork or your fingers until it begins to clump together like a bunch of math nerds at a school dance.

5. Using your fingers and the palms of your hands, press the dough against the sides and bottom of the pie plate. (If you dip your hands in flour before doing this, you won't be picking little bits of dough off your clothes for the next two days. Trust me on this.)

6. Prebake the crust for 10 minutes, then let it cool for about 10 minutes.

7. While the crust is baking and cooling, empty the yams and syrup into a large bowl. Mash yams with a potato-bug masher (or a potato masher, if you must). Then beat in the brown sugar with an electric mixer until syrupy yams look just like gooey puréed potato bugs.

8. Add the cinnamon, nutmeg, allspice, and salt.

9. Beat in the eggs until they cry for mercy, and then beat in the evaporated milk. (I never realized cooking was so violent.)

10. Pour the filling into the crust and bake the pie for about 50 minutes. By this time, you should be starving.

11. You can tell the pie is done if you jiggle it and the center moves with the rest of the pie.

Notes

 If you toss a cat out of a car window, does it become kitty litter?

12. Put the pie onto a cooling rack for about 10 minutes. Slice and top each piece with whipped cream. Eat.

Oops. You were supposed to save the pie to sweeten up your contact. Oh well. Time to bake another one.

Notes

 If a cow laughs, does milk come out her nose?

Now, uh, where were we? Oh yeah—information sources.

Records

They're boring, I know, but useful. A document is like physical evidence—you can read it, copy it, put it on a CD, maybe even stuff it in your pocket. And records are available to anyone who knows where to look. You can find them in file cabinets, in desk drawers, on the secretary's computer, or on the stereo (if your parents have an old-fashioned one).

Records can tell a lot about your suspect's history—like how often she's been to the principal's office, or whether he was absent on a particular day, or whether his grades are scraping the bottom of the barrel.

Paging Chet Gecko!

I get my hands on most document records either by sneaking around or by cozying up to a secretary. Either way, you gotta be careful not to get caught at it.

Notes

 If I'm a nobody, and nobody's perfect, does that mean I'm perfect?

Dumpster Diving

If you don't know what you're looking for, you have a good chance of finding it. After all, there's lots of interesting stuff out there to look at. It's only when you want something *specific* that the going gets hard.

Dumpster diving is a great example of this. If you're looking for just one thing in all the trash that's in a Dumpster, you'll have a hard time (unless you're looking to stink to high heaven). But if you plow through the pile with an open mind—and a closed mouth—you're bound to get lucky.

Just be sure to do your Dumpster diving before lunch, 'cause leftovers can really stain your fancy duds. Here are a few things you might find in the trash:

- report cards
- test answers
- flies
- personal letters (always a source of juicy info)
- half-eaten cookies (be sure to smell before tasting)
- receipts
- maggots

Notes

Being a private eye means taking lots of guesses and hoping they turn out right. But then, so does science class.

- phone bills (find out who your suspect's been calling)
- rotten eggs (avoid at all costs)
- other detectives (hey, it's a popular place to investigate)

Notes

Sometimes detective work can be harder than a week-old sowbug biscuit.

>>Cool Trick #4

Glass Ear Say you really want to know what a suspect is saying to another shady character in the next room, but the door is closed. Fear not. Just get an ordinary water glass,* put one end up against the door and the other against your ear, and—voilà! Their secrets are revealed!

***Important tip:** Drink the water before using the glass.

Notes

If it doesn't look _natural_ and it doesn't act super, why do they call it _supernatural?_

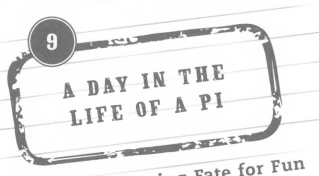

9
A DAY IN THE LIFE OF A PI

» Tempting Fate for Fun and Profit

Now that you've started to get the hang of detective work, you're probably wondering: What does a private eye's day look like? Well, it looks pretty much like anyone else's day, except that it's packed with danger, suspense, close calls, and adventure. (And that's just the time spent trying to stay out of class.)

Here's a typical day's schedule:

7:00 A.M.   Alarm clock rings. Hit snooze button.

7:10   Detective's mother calls. Ignore her.

7:15   Alarm rings again. Whack it with pillow.

7:30   Mom pulls detective out of bed by tail. Get up.

Notes

If you can pick your friends, and you can pick your nose...why can't you pick your friend's nose?

7:35 Morning activities: brushing teeth, showering, etc.

7:55 Sit down to nutritious meal of cricket hotcakes, krangleberry yogurt, fruit, juice, pillbug muffins, centipede breakfast bars, Krispy Kockroach cereal, chocolate-glazed dragonfly crullers, etc.

8:00 Finish breakfast.

8:05 Leave for school.

8:10 Return for homework. Leave for school again.

8:15 School starts.

Notes

There are two theories on how to argue with a principal. Neither one works.

8:20	Arrive at school. Create note for tardy excuse.
8:25–10:00	Pure boredom (also known as schoolwork).
10:00–10:15	Recess. Meet with partner and client. Interview suspect #1; discover he has short fuse. Hide from suspect #1 until recess ends.
10:15–11:00	Stupefying boredom (more schoolwork). Observe suspect #2 passing notes to another classmate. Try intercepting note. Get busted by teacher.
11:05	Trip to principal's office. Enlightening discussion with principal. He offers to enroll detective in the Frequent Detention Plan. Detective declines offer.
11:15–11:40	Excruciating boredom (more schoolwork).
11:45	Lunch. Hearty meal of happy-spider lasagna, maggot macaroni cakes, sowbug rolls, dandelion salad, and butterscotch earwig pudding. Detective scores seconds, thanks to inside connection.
11:50	Finish lunch. Meet partner and tail suspect #2 around playground.

Notes

 Let a smile be your umbrella...and you'll get a mouthful of rain.

	Observe suspect talking with known gang members. Sneak up on gang meeting.
12:00 noon	Detective's partner sneezes. Meeting adjourns. Partner and detective adjourn, too—at top speed.
12:00–12:10 P.M.	Exercise period. Detective and partner practice running, climbing, and flying around school, aided by gang members.
12:10–12:15	Recovery period. While resting, interview librarian regarding latest supernatural happenings at school.
12:15–1:05	Total monotony. (Yeah, that's right: schoolwork.) Request bathroom break; spend it investigating suspect #1's locker.
1:15	Recess. Second exercise period begins when suspect #1 unexpectedly returns to locker. Detective investigates Dumpster as hiding place. Unexpected clue turns up in garbage.
1:30–2:15	Mind-numbing dullness. Boredom slightly relieved when classmate sets fire to science project.
2:15	School ends. Meet with partner to discuss leads. Rooftop stakeout of second gang meeting. Disappointing

Notes

 Trouble stuck to him like dumb on a dingbat.

results: no suspects, no illegal activity, no snacks.

3:15 Return to home office. Consume health snacks—sweet potato-bug pie, boll weevil biscuits, pillbug crunch bars, mantis milk, and cinnamon tapeworm crisps.

3:20 Finish snacks. Discuss cases with partner.

3:30 Repel infiltration attempt by sister.

3:45 Practice self-defense moves until snacks threaten to make reappearance. Work on new codes and ciphers. Maintain disguise kits.

4:15 Repel second infiltration attempt by sister.

4:16 Unscheduled visit by detective's mother. Partner heads home.

4:20–5:00 Cruel torture (homework assignments).

5:00 Detective ends workday. Eat dinner, read comic books, watch TV, avoid bedtime.

9:00 Lights out.

Notes

 Things are darkest just before...they go completely black.

As a special bonus, here's Mrs. Bagoong's recipe for Maggot Macaroni Cakes, one of the highlights of cafeteria cooking. Accept no substitutes.

MAGGOT MACARONI CAKES*

*This one involves sharp knives. Better be supervised by a trained commando, Green Beret, or similar adult.

Makes 12 cakes
Total preparation time: 1 hour and 10 minutes

Macaroni Cakes

1 Tbsp. olive oil
½ small onion, carefully sliced really thin
3 cloves garlic, minced
1 Tsp. dried oregano (or 1 Tbsp. fresh, minced)

½ Tsp. chili powder (optional, not for wussies)
1 or 2 Tbsp. hot sauce (optional, ditto)
1 Tsp. salt
¼ Tsp. pepper

1½ cups dried elbow macaroni
¼ cup fresh bread crumbs (or 2 Tbsp. dried crumbs)

2¼ cups water

1 egg
2 cups shredded cheese (any color, but orange looks nice)
1 green onion, sliced into little round disks

Notes

Never take on a wacko for a client. It wastes your time and it annoys the wacko.

Maggoty Topping

2 Tbsp. olive oil

$3/4$ cup maggots (or you can use puffed brown rice cereal, which looks a lot like maggots and tastes almost as good)

$1/4$ cup fresh bread crumbs (or 2 Tbsp. dried crumbs)

2 Tsp. seasoned salt

Cooking Tools and Materials

knife for slicing and chopping

2-quart saucepan that can be used on the stove top and in the oven; must have lid

1 set of measuring cups

1 set of measuring spoons

large spoon or spatula for stirring

Notes

Danger is my business, but dessert is my delight.

1 small jar with lid

cheese grater (if not using shredded cheese)

1 medium skillet

nonstick cooking spray

12-muffin pan

hot pads

Mighty Maggot comic book (to read if cooking gets boring)

Preheat the oven to 350 degrees.

1. *Pour olive oil into a 2-quart saucepan that can be used on the stove top and in the oven. Place over medium heat on the stove top. Add the thinly sliced onion, minced garlic, and oregano.*

2. *Stir in the chili powder, hot sauce, salt, and pepper.*

3. *Stir in the macaroni (uncooked) and bread crumbs. Mix all ingredients together.*

4. *Stir in water. Just keep on stirring until you go stir crazy.*

5. *When the water begins to boil, put the lid on saucepan and pop pan into oven. Set your timer for 15 minutes.*

6. *While the macaroni mixture is baking, break egg into a small jar, put the lid on the jar REALLY TIGHT, and shake the jar really hard to break up the egg and mix the egg white and yolk together. (Also, it helps if you don't put the shells in the jar. Trust me on this.)*

7. *Grate the cheese if it is not already shredded, and slice the green onion.*

8. *For the topping: Heat 2 Tbsp. of olive oil in a medium skillet over medium heat.*

9. *Pour the maggots (or puffed rice) and bread crumbs into the skillet and stir in the seasoned salt. Make sure none of the maggots have changed into flies—flies ruin the flavor.*

Notes

What if the hokey-pokey really _is_ what it's all about?

10. Stir this mess until the crumbs and maggots (or puffed rice) absorb the oil. Turn off the heat and let this maggoty topping cool.

11. Spray the inside of the muffin pan with nonstick cooking spray.

12. When your timer rings, use hot pads to take the pan out of the oven. Be careful to set it onto a hot pad so it doesn't burn the countertop or table. (Ask me how I know about that one. On second thought, don't.)

13. Remove the lid of the saucepan carefully. A lot of hot steam will billow out when you take off the lid, so keep your face away from the pan.

14. Stir the egg, cheese, and green onions into the baked macaroni mixture.

15. Use the $\frac{1}{3}$-cup measure to scoop the macaroni mixture into the muffin pan.

16. Sprinkle 1 Tbsp. of the maggoty topping onto the top of each macaroni cake.

17. Put the muffin pan into the oven and set the timer for another 10 minutes.

18. When the timer rings again, remove the muffin pan and let it sit for about 10 minutes to cool. Don't cheat, now.

19. Put each cake onto a plate and serve to your family or friends. Sprinkle any leftover maggoty topping around on each plate to make the cakes look yummier. Guaranteed, your family will never ask you to cook again.

111

Notes

My idea of a balanced diet is a cookie in each hand.

10
DISGUISE IN LOVE WITH YOU

» Undercover Work

While investigating, a detective spends most of his time on the outside looking in. We're always trying to figure out the how, who, why, when, where, and what-the-heck? But sometimes the only way to crack a case is the way a chick cracks an egg—from the inside.

Hey! It's sexist to call a girl a chick. And we don't crack eggs any differently from guys.

I was talking about a newborn baby birdie.

Oh. Never mind.

Notes

 Whoever said you can't have your case and eat it, too, never met Chet Gecko.

Undercover work gives you the inside view. Whether you're joining a bunch of smugglers or pretending to be a member of the chess club, you can learn things undercover that you can't learn any other way.

See, when people think you belong to their group, they open up. Also, when you're on the spot, you're more likely to notice clues and suspicious behavior.

But undercover work carries more risk than a possum has fleas. Think you can handle it? Take this quick quiz and find out.

Notes

A tough private eye can resist anything...
except temptation.

If you're undercover in a gang of crooks, and they find out you're really a double agent, they will:

a. say "Oh, darn that crafty detective," and let you go;
b. surrender gladly, because you have the goods on them;
c. gnash their teeth;
d. find new and interesting ways to decorate your head with a tire iron.

If you chose anything other than *d,* maybe this is not the job for you. You might want to investigate a career in cheese management.

However, if you're tough enough to handle undercover work, study these tips (but don't write them on your palm). An undercover detective:

- **is a good actor.** Does this mean you should memorize *Hamlet* or try out for the school play? No. (Unless your teacher forces you to—and even then you should put up a fight.)

  But when you're undercover, you have to pretend to be someone you're not. You've gotta speak differently, talk differently, and even *act* differently.

*That's no problem for you. You act really different*ly.

Funny.

114

Notes

If quitters never win and winners never quit, who came up with the saying, "quit while you're ahead"?

- **keeps his cool.** You never know what's gonna happen, and you have to stay calm—even if you're surprised or scared. If your suspect says, "Let's go kidnap the principal," act like you're a criminal, too.

  Wrong: "Oh, mercy me! But that's dangerous and illegal."

  Right: "Yeah, and let's snatch the vice principal while we're at it."

- **knows what he's after.** If you don't have a clear idea of what you're looking for, you end up wasting more time than an earthworm taking flying lessons. Plus, if you're not watching for the right thing, it could happen right under your nose and you wouldn't even know it.

That reminds me of a joke: What do you call Rudolph when he goes blind?

Okay, what?

No eye deer. Get it?

Yeah, but I wish I hadn't.

- **plays the right character.** If you're trying to infiltrate a band of deranged killer clowns and you

Notes

My workout philosophy has always been a simple one: No pain, no pain.

pose as a bank teller, do you think they'll fall for it? Probably not. (Unless they're *really* deranged.) To be accepted by morons, act like a moron.

Don't even think about commenting on that, Natalie.

- **leaves vital papers at home.** The last thing you want is for the bad guys to find something on you that blows your cover. So leave behind:
  - your detective ID badge;
  - your miniature tape recorder;
  - your notes on the case;
  - a business card from the nearest police station; and
  - that letter from the principal that says, "Thanks for going undercover and breaking up this evil band of thugs."

Dangers of Undercover Work

Going undercover is one of the riskiest things a detective can do (especially if someone has just farted under

Notes

 I like exercise. I could sit and watch other people do it all day.

the covers). We face both physical and emotional danger, and it's best to know that up front.

Physical Risks

An undercover PI faces threats from all sides. Say you've infiltrated a gang of thieves. Danger can come from three sources (four, if you count your parents):

1. **Crooks:** If the thieves somehow find out you're a detective, they might mince you into tiny bits and bake you into a pie, or fit you for a pair of concrete galoshes and drop you in the ocean. Or they might do something serious.

2. **The law:** When the cops (or school authorities) bust the gang in the middle of a theft, how can they tell you're not a thug? After all, you look like a thief and smell like a thief. Thinking about wearing a pin on your coat that reads, *Actually a Good Guy?* See item 1 above.

3. **Innocent bystanders:** If you and the gang are hotfooting it out of a warehouse, loaded down with stolen earwax candles, how can an ordinary citizen tell you're not a thief? He or she might decide to play hero, whomping you over the head with a whiffle-ball bat. And believe me, that smarts.

Notes

 Who do you think put the "art" in "smart aleck"?

Emotional Risks

After you've spent three weeks living, sleeping, and thieving with a band of evil ferrets, you might start thinking like a ferret, too. You might even start believing the bad guys are your friends. Big mistake.

Other emotional dangers? Um…well, you might get a headache trying to keep your cover story straight.

That shouldn't be a problem for you.

What do you mean?

With all the excuse notes you've written? You're a pro.

Aw, you're too kind.

Notes

Principal Zero was the kind of guy who would stuff your mouth full of tardy slips, then paddle your behind for mumbling.

11
THAT'S WHAT ENDS ARE FOR

» The Last Word

So now you know everything you need to be a detective. That means there'll be lots more detectives out there now.

Hmm. Maybe I shouldn't have written this book after all.

Of course, even if you *do* become a PI, there's no guarantee you'll be a hotshot like Natalie and me. It took us years of practice, luck, and patient study to get to be so good.

Plus, you write up our case studies, so you can cut out our goofs.

Yes, there is that.

Notes

 Some people can tell what time it is by looking at the sun, but I've never been able to make out the numbers.

Anyway, I can't think of any other important stuff to tell you. You're on your own from here. Close the book. Go home.

What about some helpful lists and forms to start them on their way?

Geez, a guy might think you actually want the competition.

Notes

Acting is all about honesty. If you can fake that, you've got it made.

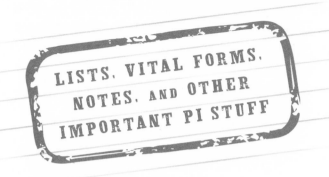

LISTS, VITAL FORMS, NOTES, AND OTHER IMPORTANT PI STUFF

Checklist: What Every Detective Needs

__ magnifying glass

__ cool hat

__ office

__ PI license

__ disguise kit

__ fingerprint kit

__ snappy comebacks

__ notepad and pencil

__ camera

__ cool detective-type name

__ snacks

__ *a smart partner*

Notes

The case was more tangled than a pair of pythons on a hot date.

Detective Lingo

If you want to walk the walk, you've gotta learn how to talk the talk. Scope out this detective lingo, and you'll be talking like a real peeper in no time.

bad egg/bad apple the kind of guy or girl that spoils the whole barrel

Big House jail, or detention hall

boingo the story, the happenings

Unh-uh, that's not a word.

dame what we private eyes call a girl

dive a low-down, cheap place (like Murray's House of Crud)

duck soup easy, a piece of cake (*Hmm*, that reminds me...)

finger, put the finger on identify

goon thug, tough guy

grill to question someone

gumshoe a detective (especially when we don't watch where we walk)

hoof it to walk

122

Notes

A day without chocolate is like a day without sunshine. And a day without sunshine is like... night.

hoosegow See *Big House.*

kisser mouth

Can I get cooties by writing this?

lug See *mook.*

mook See *mug.*

mug a big tough guy; also, your face

packing heat carrying a weapon (like a rubberband gun)

patsy a fall guy; someone who takes the blame, a fool

peeper what the bad guys call a detective

PI cherry, please. Just kidding. PI is short for private investigator.

put the screws on to get tough with

ringer a fake

rumtiddly-poo acting like a loony bird

That's not a word, either.

sap a dumb guy; also, a blackjack (beanbaglike weapon)

123

Notes

 If you toss a cat out of a car window, does it become kitty litter?

schnozz your beak, your beezer, your nose

shadowing sneaking around and following someone

snitch a low-down weasel (or other animal) who tattles on someone

snoop a detective (We have lots of nicknames, huh?)

stool pigeon someone who tattles (not necessarily a bird)

tail to follow someone (also, that thing hanging off your tuckus)

tail job an assignment to follow someone around

tighten the screws put pressure on somebody

trap mouth

tuckus the part of the body your tail hangs from

wilmerino a slow-witted person

Come on, Chet. Get real.

wrong-o a bad guy (or girl)

Notes

 If a cow laughs, does milk come out her nose?

Forms Every Detective Can Use

✂ ---

EXCUSE SLIP

Please excuse _____ from school/class today because he/she:

___had a brain malfunction.

___caught a fever from a moldy yak.

___hasn't done the homework.

___has been asked to appear on _____ (TV show).

___grew an extra nose and had to have it surgically removed.

___superglued himself/herself to a migrating wildebeest.

Don't bother trying to call me to check this information. Our telephone was swallowed by a deranged plumber.

Sincerely,

_____

(Illegible scrawl goes here.)

Notes

 If I'm a nobody, and nobody's perfect, does that mean I'm perfect?

DETECTIVE LICENSE

This is to certify that _____ is a real, honest-to-goodness private eye. No kidding. He/she has passed a bunch of secret tests that we're not allowed to tell you about. (That's why they're secret.)

This person is of high moral fiber (ha!), sound mind (we wish), and possesses razor-sharp detective skills (we hope he/she doesn't cut himself/herself).

Anyway, he/she has passed all of our tests; we've taken his/her money; and we can't figure out what else to do with her/him. So I guess they've graduated.

Witnessed this day, the _____ of _____.
(date)   (month)

_____
Random Chaunce, President of Flimflam Detective School

_____
(your name here)

FLIMFLAM

Notes

Being a private eye means taking lots of guesses and hoping they turn out right. But then, so does science class.

SEARCH WARRANT

We hereby declare that it's okay for this detective, _____, to come search your home/office/room/luggage— even if he or she happens to toss around your stuff, break your favorite plates, eat your cookies, and otherwise behave like Hurricane Carlito. Really, it's fine with us. (We don't have to clean up the mess.)

If you have any problem with this, or any questions, please call us at the number below.

_____

(Illegible, smeared name and phone number)

Notes

Sometimes detective work can be harder than a week-old sowbug biscuit.

PRIVATE EYE

No case too small,
no snack too big.

Notes

If it doesn't look _natural_ and it doesn't act _super_, why do they call it _supernatural_?

Read all of the mysteries from
the Tattered Casebook of Chet Gecko
in hardcover and paperback.

CASE #1 THE CHAMELEON WORE CHARTREUSE

Some cases start rough, some cases start easy. This one started with a dame. (That's what we private eyes call a girl.) She was cute and green and scaly. She looked like trouble and smelled like...grasshoppers.

Shirley Chameleon came to me when her little brother, Billy, turned up missing. (I suspect she also came to spread cooties, but that's another story.) She turned on the tears. She promised me some stinkbug pie. I said I'd find the brat.

But when his trail led to a certain stinky-breathed, bad-tempered, jumbo-sized Gila monster, I thought I'd bitten off more than I could chew. Worse, I had to chew fast: If I didn't find Billy in time, it would be bye-bye, stinkbug pie.

CASE #2 THE MYSTERY OF MR. NICE

How would you know if some criminal mastermind tried to impersonate your principal? My first clue: He was nice to me.

This fiend tried everything—flattery, friendship, food—but he still couldn't keep me off the case. Natalie and I followed a trail of clues as thin as the cheese on a cafeteria hamburger. And we found a ring of corruption that went from the janitor right up to Mr. Big.

In the nick of time, we rescued Principal Zero and busted up the PTA meeting, putting a stop to the evil genius. And what

Notes

If you can pick your friends, and you can pick your nose...why can't you pick your friend's nose?

thanks did we get? Just the usual. A cold handshake and a warm soda.

But that's all in a day's work for a private eye.

CASE #3 FAREWELL, MY LUNCHBAG

If danger is my business, then dinner is my passion. I'll take any case if the pay is right. And what pay could be better than Mothloaf Surprise?

At least that's what I thought. But in this particular case, I bit off more than I could chew.

Cafeteria lady Mrs. Bagoong hired me to track down whoever was stealing her food supplies. The long, slimy trail led too close to my own backyard for comfort.

And much, much too close to the very scary Jimmy "King" Cobra. Without the help of Natalie Attired and our school janitor, Maureen DeBree, I would've been gecko sushi.

CASE #4 THE BIG NAP

My grades were lower than a salamander's slippers, and my bank account was trying to crawl under a duck's belly. So why did I take a case that didn't pay anything?

Put it this way: Would *you* stand by and watch some evil power turn *your* classmates into hypnotized zombies? (If that wasn't just what normally happened to them in math class, I mean.)

My investigations revealed a plot meaner than a roomful of rhinos with diaper rash.

Someone at Emerson Hicky was using a sinister video game to put more and more students into la-la land. And it was up to

Notes

There are two theories on how to argue with a principal. Neither one works.

me to stop it, pronto—before that someone caught up with me, and I found myself taking the Big Nap.

CASE #5 THE HAMSTER OF THE BASKERVILLES

Elementary school is a wild place. But this was ridiculous. Someone—or some*thing*—was tearing up Emerson Hicky. Classrooms were trashed. Walls were gnawed. Mysterious tunnels riddled the playground like worm chunks in a pan of earthworm lasagna.

But nobody could spot the culprit, let alone catch him.

I don't believe in the supernatural. My idea of voodoo is my mom's cockroach-ripple ice cream.

Then, a teacher reported seeing a monster on full-moon night, and I got the call.

At the end of a twisted trail of clues, I had to answer the burning question: Was it a vicious, supernatural were-hamster on the loose, or just another Science Fair project gone wrong?

CASE #6 THIS GUM FOR HIRE

Never thought I'd see the day when one of my worst enemies would hire me for a case. Herman the Gila Monster was a sixth-grade hoodlum with a first-rate left hook. He told me someone was disappearing the football team, and he had to put a stop to it. *Big whoop.*

He told me he was being blamed for the kidnappings, and he had to clear his name. *Boo hoo.*

Then he said that I could either take the case and earn a nice reward, or have my face rearranged like a bargain-basement Picasso painted by a spastic chimp.

I took the case.

Notes

 Let a smile be your umbrella...and you'll get a mouthful of rain.

But before I could find the kidnapper, I had to go undercover. And that meant facing something that scared me worse than a chorus line of criminals in steel-toed boots: P.E. class.

CASE #7 THE MALTED FALCON

It was tall, dark, and chocolaty—the stuff dreams are made of. It was a treat so titanic that nobody had been able to finish one single-handedly (or even single-mouthedly). It was the Malted Falcon.

How far would you go for the ultimate dessert? Somebody went too far, and that's where I came in.

The local sweets shop held a contest. The prize: a year's supply of free Malted Falcons. Some lucky kid scored the winning ticket. She brought it to school for show-and-tell.

But after she showed it, somebody swiped it. And no one would tell where it went.

Following a strong hunch and an even stronger sweet tooth, I tracked the ticket through a web of lies more tangled than a rattlesnake doing the rumba. But the time to claim the prize was fast approaching. Would the villain get the sweet treat—or his just desserts?

CASE #8 TROUBLE IS MY BEESWAX

Okay, I confess. When test time rolls around, I'm as tempted as the next lizard to let my eyeballs do the walking...to my neighbor's paper.

But Mrs. Gecko didn't raise no cheaters. (Some language manglers, perhaps.) So when a routine investigation uncovered a test-cheating ring at Emerson Hicky, I gave myself a new case: Put the cheaters out of business.

Notes

 Trouble stuck to him like dumb on a dingbat.

Easier said than done. Those double-dealers were slicker than a frog's fanny and twice as slimy.

Oh, and there was one other small problem: The finger of suspicion pointed to two dames. The ringleader was either the glamorous Lacey Vail, or my own classmate Shirley Chameleon.

Sheesh. The only thing I hate worse than an empty Pillbug Crunch wrapper is a case full of dizzy dames.

CASE #9 GIVE MY REGRETS TO BROADWAY

Some things you can't escape, however hard you try—like dentist appointments, visits with strange-smelling relatives, and being in the fourth-grade play. I had always left the acting to my smart-aleck pal, Natalie, but then one day it was my turn in the spotlight.

Stage fright? Me? You're talking about a gecko who has laughed at danger, chuckled at catastrophe, and sneezed at sinister plots.

I was terrified.

Not because of the acting, mind you. The script called for me to share a major lip-lock with Shirley Chameleon—Cootie Queen of the Universe!

And while I was trying to avoid that trap, a simple missing persons case took a turn for the worse—right into the middle of my play. Would opening night spell curtains for my client? And, more important, would someone invent a cure for cooties? But no matter—whatever happens, the sleuth must go on.

Notes

Things are darkest just before...they go completely black.

Some things at school you can count on. Pop quizzes always pop up just after you've spent your study time studying comics. Chef's Surprise is always a surprise, but never a good one. And no matter how much you learn today, they always make you come back tomorrow.

But sometimes, Emerson Hicky amazes you. And just like finding a killer bee in a box of Earwig Puffs, you're left shocked, stung, and discombobulated.

Foul play struck at my school; that's nothing new. But then the finger of suspicion pointed straight at my favorite fowl: Natalie Attired. Framed as a blackmailer, my partner was booted out of Emerson Hicky quicker than a hoptoad on a hot plate.

I tackled the case for free. Mess with my partner, mess with me.

Then things took a turn for the worse. Just when I thought I might clear her name, Natalie disappeared. And worse still, she left behind one clue: a reddish smear that looked kinda like the jelly from a beetle-jelly sandwich but raised an ugly question: Was it murder, or something serious?

Notes

Never take on a wacko for a client. It wastes your time and it annoys the wacko.

Notes

Danger is my business, but dessert is my delight.

Notes

What if the hokey-pokey really _is_ what it's all about?

I'm not fooling.
Close this book right now!

Don't you listen?

You opened the book—

after I told you not to!